Mireille Messier

Night Flight

Illustrated by Carl Pelletier

SCHOLASTIC CANADA LTD.

New York Toronto London Auckland Sydney
Mexico City New Delhi Hong Kong Buenos Aires

To my good friend Lisa, whose name unfortunately only rhymes with pizza.
— M. M.

For Thomas, Alexis and Mohan
— C. P.

Scholastic Canada Ltd.
604 King Street West, Toronto, Ontario M5V 1E1, Canada

Scholastic Inc.
557 Broadway, New York, NY 10012, USA

Scholastic Australia Pty Limited
PO Box 579, Gosford, NSW 2250, Australia

Scholastic New Zealand Limited
Private Bag 94407, Greenmount, Auckland, New Zealand

Scholastic Children's Books
Euston House, 24 Eversholt Street, London NW1 1DB, UK

Library and Archives Canada Cataloguing in Publication

Messier, Mireille, 1971-
[Luca. English]
Night flight / Mireille Messier ; Carl Pelletier, illustrator.

Translation of: Luca.
ISBN 978-0-545-98649-6

I. Pelletier, Carl II. Title: Luca. English.
PS8576.E7737L8313 2009 jC843'.54 C2008-907363-0

ISBN-10 0-545-98649-4

6 5 4 3 2 1 Printed in Canada 09 10 11 12 13

When he goes to bed, almost every night,
Luca is a pirate, archeologist or knight.

From his flannel galleon,
Luca leaps and roars:
"Head into the wind, me hardies!
I see dinosaurs!"

His mother sighs: "Oh, Luca,
Your head is in the clouds.
Stop this silly ruckus,
And please don't be so loud!"

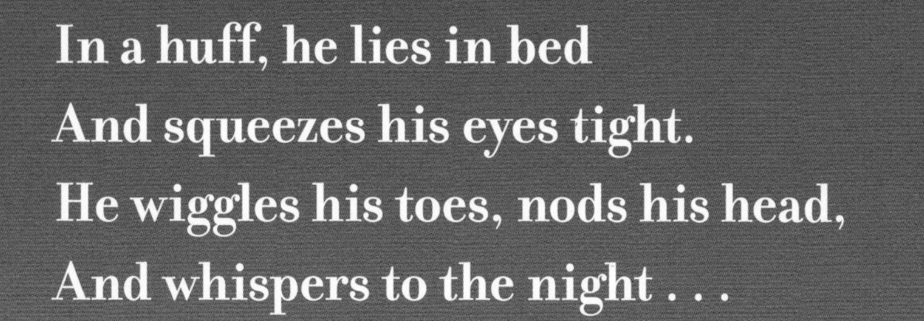

In a huff, he lies in bed
And squeezes his eyes tight.
He wiggles his toes, nods his head,
And whispers to the night . . .

Moonlight
Starlight
Twilight
Night flight!

In a second and a flash,
He's now Sir Knight of Succotash!

Luca dons a suit of armour,
Holds his shield high up,
And starts his quest for long-lost treasure
And the Stanley Cup.

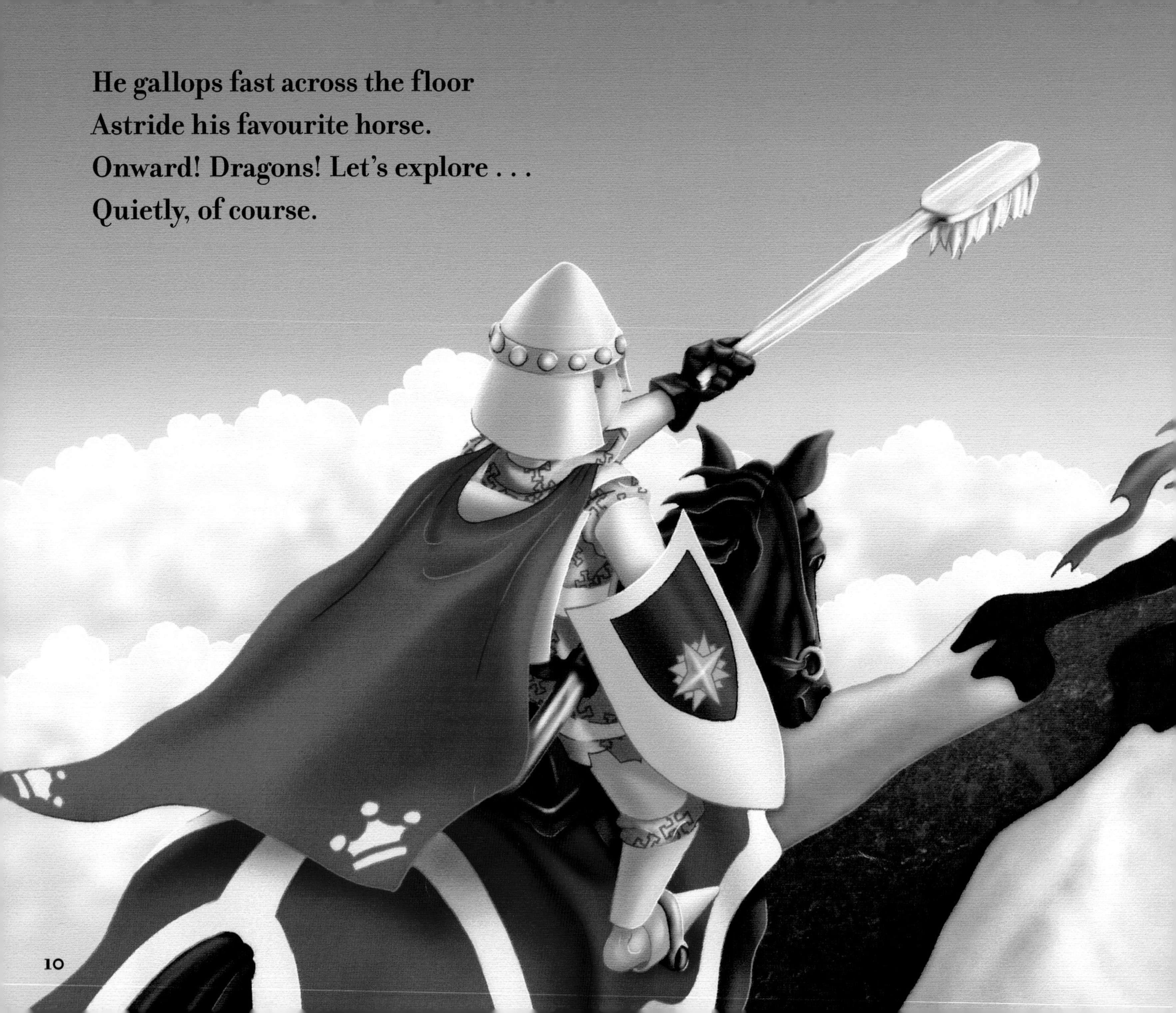

He gallops fast across the floor
Astride his favourite horse.
Onward! Dragons! Let's explore . . .
Quietly, of course.

Armed with toothbrush-sword
And draped in woolly cape,
This brave knight snares the dragon,
Leaves it no escape.

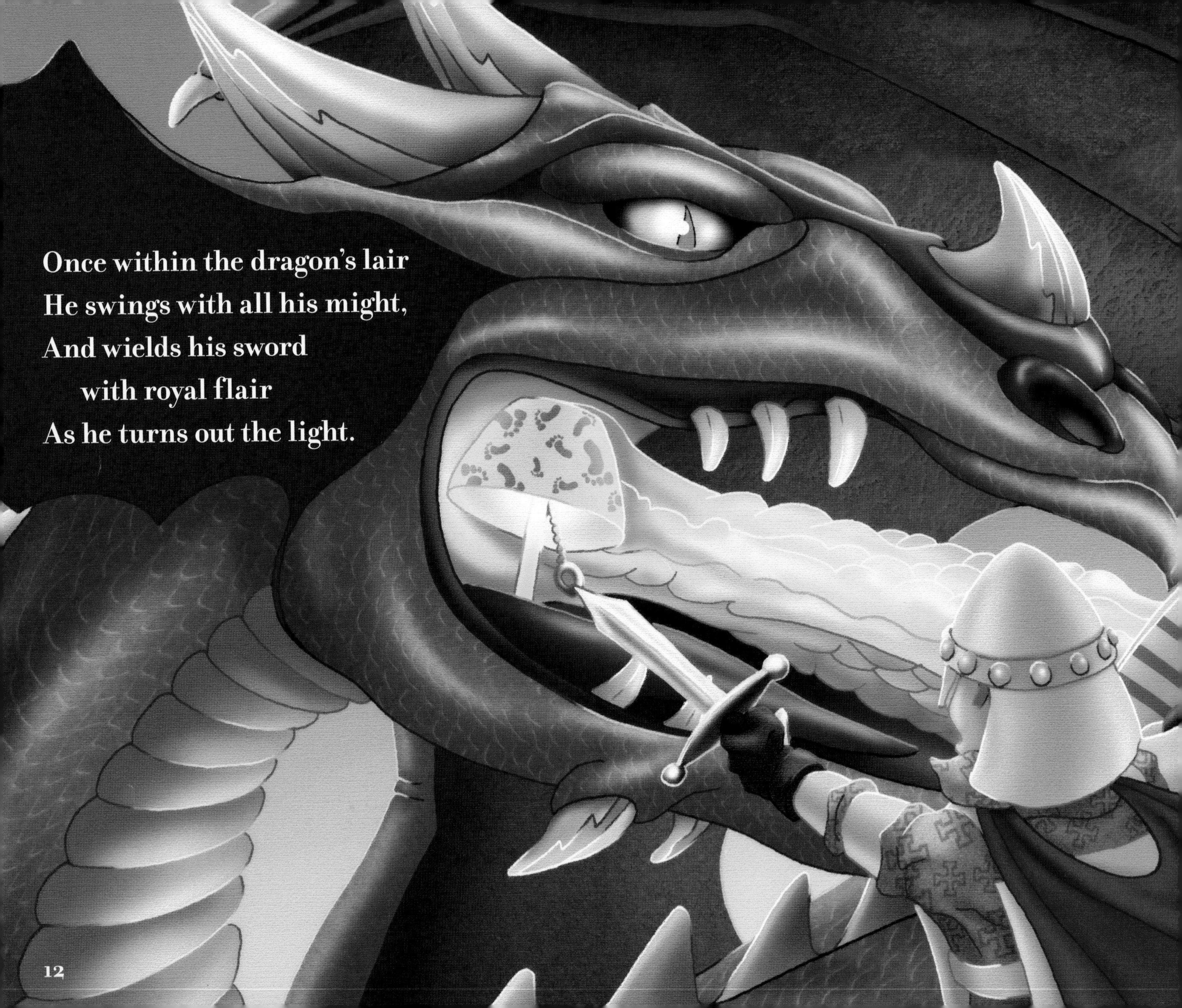

Once within the dragon's lair
He swings with all his might,
And wields his sword
with royal flair
As he turns out the light.

Beyond his sleeping chamber
A voice rumbles from the gloom:
"That's enough nonsense –
I want quiet in this room!"

His dad the king then tucks him in,
Leaves kisses on his nose,
Slays one final dragon,
And leaves on tippytoes.

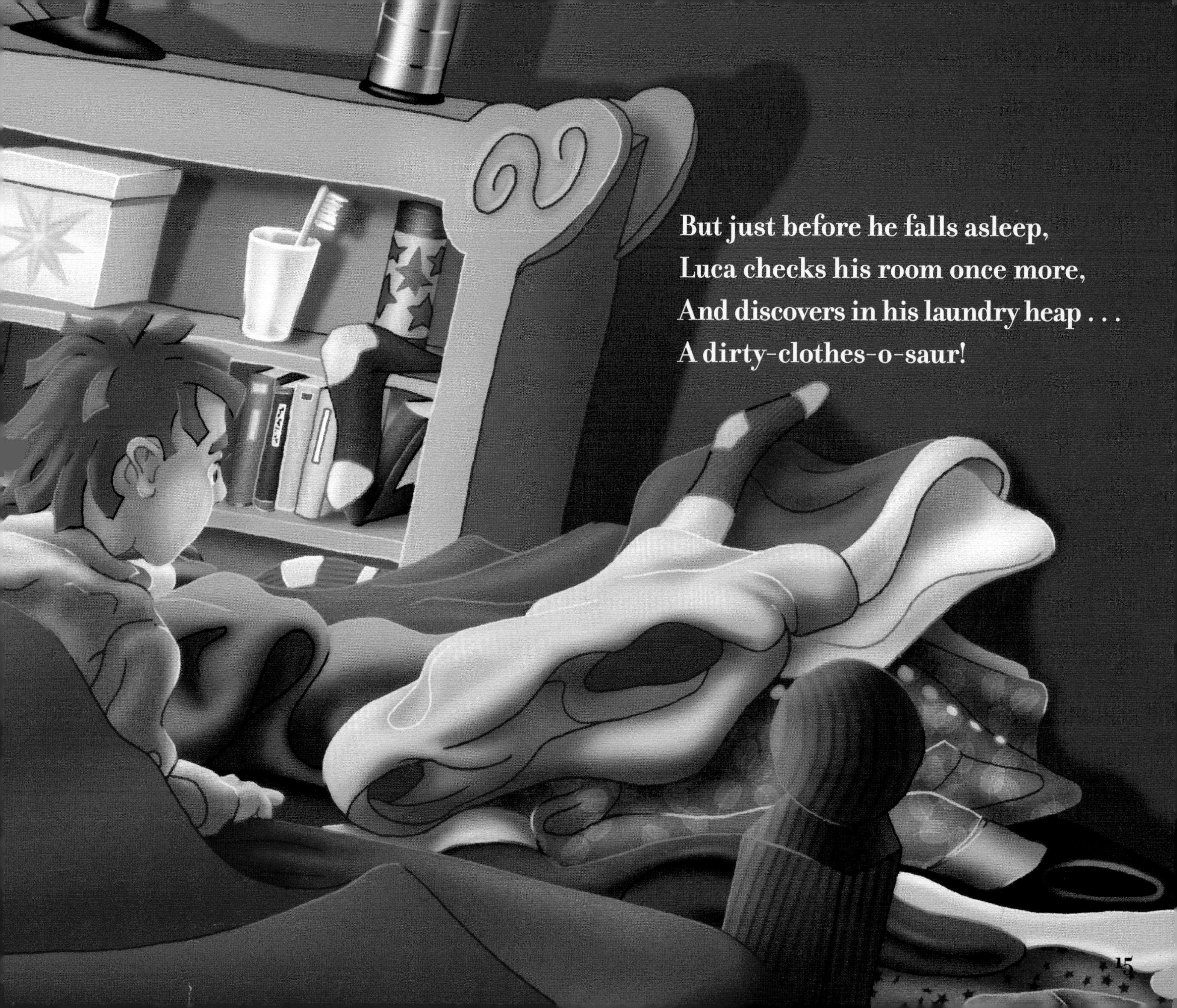

But just before he falls asleep,
Luca checks his room once more,
And discovers in his laundry heap . . .
A dirty-clothes-o-saur!

That's when...

Moonlight

Starlight

Twilight

Night flight!

In a second and a twist, he's an archeologist!

The dig begins without delay.
He shovels off the dirt.
And finds a treasure in decay,
Underneath a shirt!

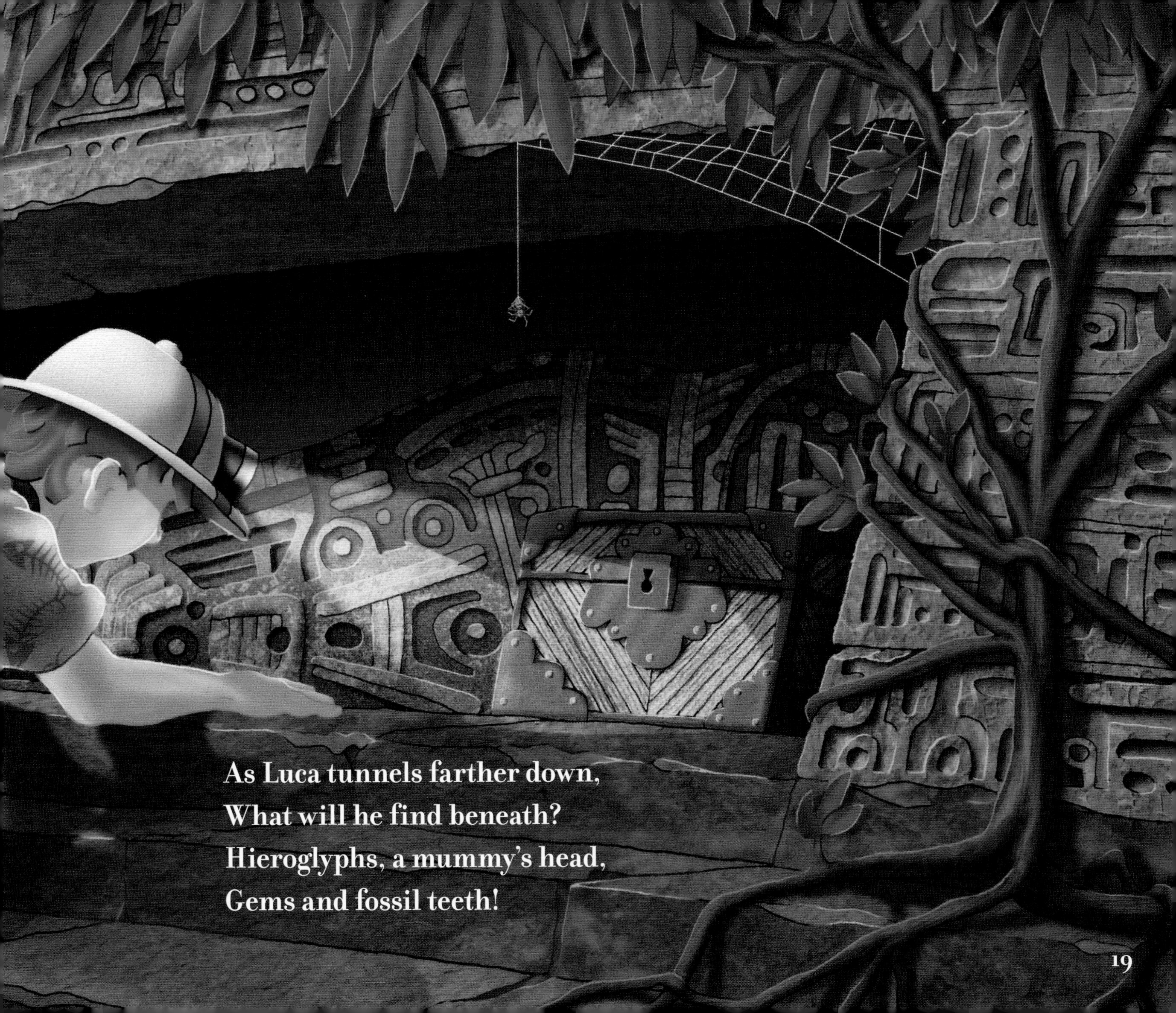

As Luca tunnels farther down,
What will he find beneath?
Hieroglyphs, a mummy's head,
Gems and fossil teeth!

Alas, his triumph will be brief.
The dig won't go ahead.
Mum, the scientist-in-chief,
Escorts him back to bed.

"It's very, very hot in here.
I'll never, ever sleep, I fear."

That's when . . .

Moonlight

Starlight

Twilight

Night flight!

In a second and a speck,
Luca's on a desert trek!

Surrounded by large dromedaries,
Blinded by the glare,
His throat is parched, his tongue is dry,
And sand gets everywhere!

The oasis down the hall
Lies in forbidden lands.
Luca has to call for help:
"Water!" he demands.

The sultan of the bathroom
Brings a goblet for his thirst,
And whispers to him softly,
"Play tomorrow. Sleep first!"

With so much water in the glass,
The tide rises all around.

That's when . . .

Moonlight

Starlight

Twilight

Night flight!

In a second and a bean,
He's captain of a submarine!

With his trusty periscope
Luca looks so brave,
Finding coral and a shipwreck
Deep beneath the waves.

Periscope down! We're under attack!
It's a giant squid!
A forehand pass, a backhand shot
Hooray for Captain Kid!

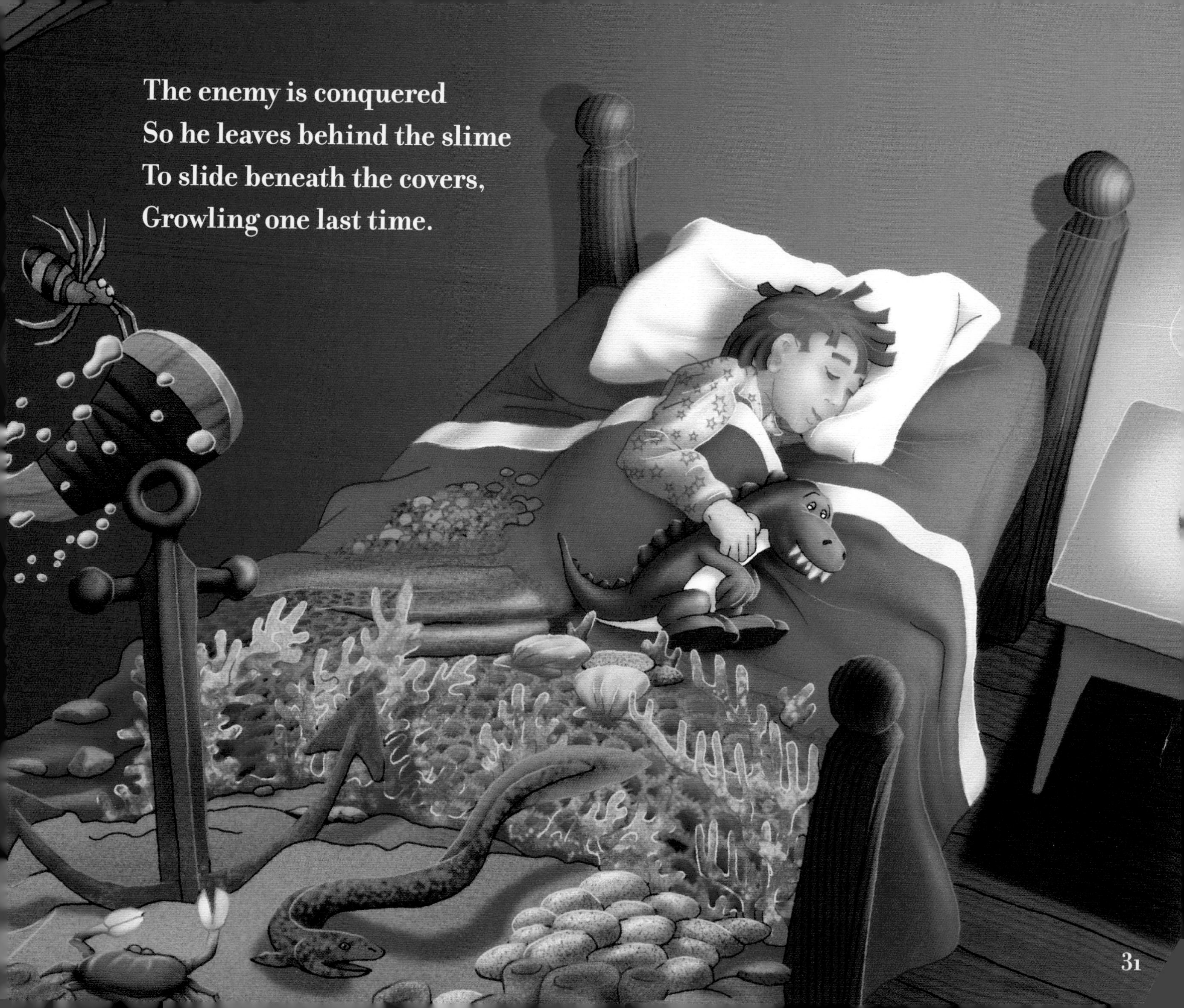

The enemy is conquered
So he leaves behind the slime
To slide beneath the covers,
Growling one last time.

"Sleep tight!" calls his father.
"Sweet dreams," says his mum.
But Captain Luca sails again . . .
Now what will he become?